Wild Beauty

Jim Connelly

Other books by Jim Connelly

Tom and Anna on the Trail: the Case of the Missing Schoolgirl (2014)

Tom and Anna in Danger: the Case of the Disappearing Dogs (2014)

Tom and Anna take a Chance: the Case of the Bungling Bird Bandits (2015)

My Folk: Four Hundred Years of Hazards, Tooths, and Connellys (2015)

Mountain Boy (2016)

Talk of the Town: Warragul/Drouin (2017)

Talk of the Town (2): Warragul/Drouin (2018)

Pickled Pieces and Rollicking Rhymes (2019)

Wild Beauty

Copyright

A CIP catalogue record for this book is available from the National Library of Australia.

First published in Australia 2019 by

James Timothy Connelly

12 Craig Street,

Warragul, Victoria, 3820

AUSTRALIA

ajcon@dcsi.net.au

In memory of Joyce Winifred Connelly, 1901-1968

'Pounding hooves among the timber; streaming flash of tail and mane,

Looming turpentines rise ghost-like in a wall.

Muffled roar of unshod horses, sure of foot and strong of limb,

As the silky evening shadows rise and fall'.

From *'With the Brumbies'* by Gary Harding

CHAPTER 1

Beauty was four months old.

She had a delicate and intelligent face. Her coat was a chestnut colour, like her mother's. On her nose she had a smudge of white.

Beauty belonged to Molly. Molly was eleven, and she loved Beauty to the depth her heart.

Beauty was the most important thing in the world to Molly.

Beauty had just been feeding from her mother, Bonny, and was standing by the railings.

Molly stroked her forehead and Beauty nuzzled into Molly's arm.

Beauty's life was about to be turned upside down – and Molly's too – but who could have foreseen it?

Beauty returned to her mother and Molly went back inside the house. Her mother was reading the newspaper. *'Illegal Shooting in National Park'*, the headline said.

The National Park lay on the upper edges of Molly's farm. It rose to the snowy peaks of the High Country. Brumbies had roamed these heights for many years, although conservationists complained they damaged the fragile mountain environment and wanted their numbers to be reduced.

Shooting is not allowed in National Parks, but if shooters were to go into the Park, they might shoot wild pigs or deer or kangaroos – or horses!

The brumbies were always at risk from illegal shooters who found fun in destroying these beautiful animals.

Molly's heart broke when she thought of the innocent creatures whose lives were in danger.

She read the newspaper article over her mother's shoulder.

The thought of the wild horses being killed was too much for her.

She ran to her room.

*   *   *

Molly goes to town each day to attend school. She is in the last year of primary school. The school bus picks her up each morning and brings her home each afternoon. It takes half an hour each way.

Molly has many friends on the bus. Her special friend is Prue, who lives on a farm farther down the road in to town.

Molly's mother, Janet, is thirty-eight years old. Her husband, Peter, Molly's father, works far away, on the off-shore oil rigs. He'd wanted to be a pilot earlier in his life, and gained his solo pilot's licence, but flying was expensive, so he'd had to give that up, and had gone to work on the rigs. Now he'd been there for ten years, since Molly was a toddler. At first he came home often, then less frequently, then not at all, though he does send money to help Janet with her expenses.

Janet works in town three days a week doing the bookwork for two of the shopkeepers there. She runs some twenty steers on her eighty acres and turns them off for fattening when they are fully grown. Then there's her horse, Bonny, and the new foal, Molly's foal, Beauty. Molly longs for the day Beauty is old enough for her to go riding with her mother, just the two of them together.

CHAPTER 2

Molly was at school the day of the shooting.

Janet was at home. She noticed that the mare and her foal were restless. They sensed something wrong, or perhaps their acute hearing had picked up unusual noises from the bushland to the north.

A single shot rang out. It was followed by another, then a volley of rifle-fire.

The shooting seemed to come from close by, on the low bushy hillside not far from her boundary fence.

Janet looked up in alarm. She thought she saw a quiver of movement, a flash of colour, as a mob of horses began to break from cover in panic.

Janet's first thought was of Molly. 'Thank heavens it's a school day,' she muttered.

But her concern soon turned to her own animals. The steers were undisturbed, but the two horses, mother and foal, began to fret. They circled anxiously around the inner yard, their nostrils dilated and their eyes staring. A sixth sense seemed to tell them their own kind were under attack.

A small mob of wild horses streamed over the brow of the hill, in full sight of the distraught woman.

Janet heard the crack of the rifle. Again and again it sounded. Two of the bush ponies fell. Janet covered her face in horror.

The mob swung down to lower ground. Now they swept along the fence that marked the boundary between the Park and the farm. A powerful bay stallion led them in their frenzied gallop.

In an instant, Janet's alarm swung closer to home. The mare and foal had broken through to the outer paddock. Their panic was the panic of the wild bush horses.

A four-strand barbed-wire fence separated them from the fleeing herd alongside. In some way inexplicable to humans, they found themselves at one with their brumby brothers and sisters. They felt within themselves the call and the terror of the wild things.

As Janet watched helplessly, the two – Bonny, then Beauty – crashed headlong through the boundary fence.

Janet's last glimpse of them was as they joined with the racing mob, Beauty hobbling in the rear. Then they were hidden from her sight as they rounded a granite spur and thundered into the farther hills.

The shooting stopped, and an unworldly silence filled the void.

*   *   *

That night the mob gathered in uneasy fear. They had chosen a level but forested area to enable quick flight if it was again needed. The dominant mare – the 'Queen' - had seen to that. The stallion had led them in their fear-crazed gallop, but it was the work of the dominant female to settle the horses down and choose a place where quick flight was possible.

Bonny and Beauty stood on the outskirts of the group. The stallion made efforts to drive them away, but 'Queenie' snarled at him until he, too, accepted the strangers, at least when they kept their distance.

Bonny had survived crashing through the barbed wire without serious injury. There were streaks of blood on her sides and rump, but they were skin-deep, and the blood had stopped flowing.

Beauty's injuries were more severe. The flesh on her left shoulder where she had breasted the wire lay open and ugly. During the mad gallop she had bled profusely, and heavy drops of blood still fell from the wound. Her young muscles had also suffered. Her left front fetlock was tender and swollen. It was vital for her to have rest, at least for some days. Bonny licked the young one's wounds.

Night came on. The horses, still trembling with shock, passed the night in ghostly stillness.

CHAPTER 3

Janet was surprised at Molly's reaction when she got home from school and learnt what had happened.

The death of the two brumbies hurt Molly deeply. She was speechless with rage and indignation. In a curious way, it made the loss of Bonny and Beauty easier for her to understand and accept.

Molly's grief at losing her beautiful foal, Beauty, was still profound, but her mind soon turned to the hope of recovering both mare and foal.

'If we leave a gap in the boundary fence, they'll come back. I just know it,' she declared. Her mother was not so hopeful. She knew more about the herd instinct in animals. Once with the wild bush horses, Janet thought, there was little likelihood of return. Not of the horses' own will.

However, she eased the child's mind. 'Maybe,' she said. 'We'll make a gap, and leave a salt lick there for them. One with trace elements. That might draw them back.'

'The cattle?' Molly asked, then answered her own question. 'We'll have to keep them out of the top paddock so they can't go through the gap into the bush.'

Despite her doubts, Janet was pleased to see Molly being so positive. 'We'll make a proper gap in the bush fence on

Saturday when you're home from school,' she replied.'
'And I'll keep the steers in the bottom paddock for now.'

* * *

Days turned into weeks, and there was no sign of the horses.

Molly's initial optimism turned into a dull ache inside her.

Janet tried to cheer her up. 'Perhaps we could buy another pony, one old enough for you to ride,' she suggested.

But Molly would have none of it. Her heart was set only on the return of her beloved Beauty, and of the mare with her.

Molly's friends noticed a change in her. Her teacher, too. Mrs O'Brien rang Janet up to talk it over.

'Molly is still doing her work well enough,' she said, 'but she's lost her spark. She stays in the classroom at play-time when the others are outside. Things like that.'

'Perhaps it will be better next year when Molly goes to High School,' Janet suggested. The Christmas holidays were about to begin.

'Perhaps,' said Mrs O'Brien, doubtfully, then added, 'Maybe a break away from home would be good for her.'

Janet said nothing about that. She knew there was little chance of the two of them taking a holiday. She needed the income from her work to keep the little family going.

Janet put the phone down and held her head in her hands.

There was only one thing that could help Molly - the return of the horses, and that was an unlikely dream.

Beauty seemed lost for ever.

And what of the men with the rifles? Janet didn't like to think of what else might happen in the days to come.

CHAPTER 4

In the wild, horses form small mobs, sometimes five or six, maybe up to a dozen. The mobs are loosely connected. Often, one or two of the horses will leave and pick up with another mob. The boss stallion is the protector and enforcer, but it is the dominant mare who is the real leader. Even the stallion accepts her will.

Queenie had been with this mob for years. None of the others dared to challenge her authority. She mated with the boss stallion in the spring breeding season, and drove away the younger females from him. As for the younger stallions, they knew their place and kept away from trouble with The Boss.

The two horses lost in the shooting were both females. Now, after their loss, Queenie's herd was made up of herself and five others, three of them males and two females. First, there was The Boss, together with two younger stallions. One of these had recently joined them from another mob higher up in the hills. He had been injured in fighting and carried a vivid red scar on the underside of his neck. The other male was the son of Queenie and The Boss. He had his father's bay roan colouring and possessed also his deep and powerful frame, though as yet it was not fully developed. Scar and Son of Boss usually grazed together, though there was bound to be trouble between them when both grew into full maturity.

The two fillies were a year apart in age. The older was the daughter of Queenie and the Boss, the sister of Son of Boss. She had her mother's bay colouring and, despite her wildness, had a pretty face, not unlike Beauty's. The younger filly had lost her mother to the marksman in the shooting. She was distinguished by a particularly shaggy coat, as her mother's had been. It would not be long before Pretty, the older one, would be taken off by a visiting stallion and linked up with another mob. Shaggy was only a yearling and would be content to run in the herd for the time being.

That night – the night of the shooting – these six horses gathered in a close circle. There was no rest, no sleeping. Their ears stood sharply, searching the darkness for more sounds of danger.

The two newcomers stood anxiously some ten metres away. How different they were! The bush ponies were smaller, their coats rougher, their legs thicker. The sense of living in a herd had been almost bred out of Bonny and Beauty by generations of domestication. Still, it was some instinct from ages past that had called them from their home paddock to join these wild things, and now they clung close to them through an inborn sense of belonging.

The night wore on. The only sounds were as different ones shifted their weight, perhaps snapping a twig underfoot.

Queenie's head was raised, her nostrils flared. The Boss shook his head uneasily. Towards morning a breeze began to stir the upper branches of the tree cover. Queenie felt it as a reassuring sign. Nature was taking its usual way. The dawn might bring some healing.

Meanwhile, Bonny continued to lick at Beauty's wounds. Tomorrow, the foal might begin to feed from her again.

*   *   *

Next morning the mob began their trek into the mountain fastnesses of the highest country. No enemy could penetrate here.

No quick movement, stopping only to snatch some feed from the open grassed areas and to drink from the shallows of the streams that ran in each gully.

The Boss led the way, but it was Queenie who decided when to rest and when to feed.

Behind the six bush horses trailed Bonny and Beauty. There was no resistance from the others, but no acceptance either. Not yet.

When the mob stopped to graze, the newcomers stopped also.

When the mob drank, the newcomers drank.

Beauty was in poor condition. Her muscles ached. Her front leg pained her at every step. Blood still seeped from the gash on her shoulder.

And she was hungry. At four months, she was not yet accustomed to grazing, and now her mother's milk, after the terror of the past twenty-four hours, had almost dried up.

Perhaps Queenie recognised the foal's weakness. She called frequent rests, especially when the horses got into the rocky ground cover on the steeper slopes.

Still Beauty struggled on. Her life depended on it.

Queenie knew where they were headed. Towards evening the mob entered a small valley on the southern side of the highest peak. There was some grass here, and water, too.

And safety. Queenie had never known humans – not even the most intrepid bush walkers – to come to this secluded spot.

The horses could rest and regain their strength and their composure.

*   *   *

Now began the process of acceptance.

When the horses finally camped in their sheltered valley, the two new ones, Bonny and Beauty, still stayed away from their bush cousins.

Beauty stretched herself prone on a grassy shelf, while her mother grazed nearby, returning to lick the young one's wounds and comfort her by standing near.

Queenie moved across to where Bonny was standing. At first, she began to engage her in mock battle, nipping her in the neck and breast, then butting her forcefully to the head and neck. It was not done in spite. Queenie was going through the ritual of establishing her superiority in the herd, her superiority over the newcomer.

It was both a welcome and a warning.

Over several days the merging of the two new arrivals with the wild herd continued. Scar and Son of Boss were the first to introduce themselves. They grazed alongside the mother, then sniffed at the foal as she lay on the ground. Bonny butted them away.

The fillies – Pretty and Shaggy – were slower to accept the two intruders. Their female instinct warned them that the two may be rivals in time to come – rivals in the herd's line of power, and rivals, also, for the attention of future mating partners.

As for The Boss, he took no apparent notice of the two. But, following Queenie's lead, he gave them no trouble.

Within a week, the eight horses were intermingling freely, if suspiciously.

With the mob settled down after their trauma, Queenie began to lead them to farther parts of the bush where they could find new growth to feed on.

By now, Beauty had begun to recover. She was picking some blades of grass, and was able to move herself more freely to the water to drink. In a matter of days, she was weaned – and this helped her mother also to recover her full strength.

Before long it was hard to tell Bonny and Beauty from the bush horses they had joined.

Did the thoughts of the newcomers wander to the lush paddocks and the warm hay they had once known?

And to the love of a girl who still yearned for their return?

*   *   *

The holidays had come, but it was a sad time for Molly. Her thoughts kept returning to her lost foal. Her eyes swept the edge of the forest in the forlorn hope of seeing the two horses there once again.

Christmas came and went.

The gap in the Park fence was closed up, and the cattle returned to the top paddock. It was as though the last hope of the horses' return had gone.

CHAPTER 5

Some months had passed.

Two men on horses rode casually through the scrub.

The horses were fine animals – quarter horses, bred for speed and to stay.

They were in the foothills of the National Park, a kilometre or two from Molly's farm. The heat of the summer was over and they had come planning to catch one of the brumbies that roamed the bush - or two, if they were lucky.

'Ours for the taking!' called Bob, the older of the two. His companion grunted a reply.

Both men carried coiled ropes attached to their saddles. Each rope had a knotted circle at the end, designed to be thrown over the head of another horse running alongside. In that way, it could be brought to a standstill.

Bob was a skilled bushman. He examined the ground for signs of wild horses.

'Here,' he called, suddenly, 'Hoofmarks.'

The men pulled up. 'Looks like a small mob. Maybe a dozen, maybe less,' said Bob.

The younger man, Jeff, nodded.

'Are you sure we're allowed to do this?' asked Jeff. 'Take horses out of the Park without permission?'

Bob dismissed his partner's doubts. 'Who's to stop us? There's none of the rangers around. And wouldn't they want these horses got rid of? Out of the Park?'

Jeff did not answer. He knew of the damage the horses were said to cause in the High Country.

They rode on in silence, looking for more signs of the brumbies. Now they were getting into higher and steeper country. In a boggy patch, Bob dismounted. 'They've been through here,' he declared. 'Hoofmarks everywhere. Fresh, too. This morning, I reckon, they've been here.'

Bob continued to examine the hoof prints. 'Seven or eight of them, I'd say. And they're not far away,' he added.

Bob was watching his own horse, and Jeff's, too. Both were sniffing the air. One of them began to paw the ground.

'They know,' said Bob. 'They're cunning beggars. They can smell other horses for miles around.'

The two men rode on, into steeper country, deeper into the bush, their senses on full alert.

Jeff spotted the mob first. He made a sign to Bob, and pointed into the shadows of a clump of stunted trees and bracken some hundreds of yards in front of them.

The two men drew up their horses. The mob stood stock still, staring at the intruders. Bob quickly assessed the situation. They were in scrubby country with steeper, rocky country above them.'

'They won't head there.' He spoke in a whisper. 'They'll head along the flank of this hill towards that bush country.' He pointed to some densely-forested country half a kilometre ahead of them. 'Not too bad. Gives us a chance.'

The mob stood without a trace of movement. But only for a moment.

Queenie tossed her head and spun around. The big stallion, The Boss, reared up and charged off in the direction of the tall timber. The mob followed at full speed - Queenie, the two young stallions, Scar and Son of Boss, the fillies, Pretty and Shaggy, and in the midst of them, side by side, raced Bonny and young Beauty, all tearing at breakneck speed through the scrub.

Not far behind thundered the two pursuers, their mounts closing with every stride.

* * *

Beauty raced shoulder to shoulder with her mother. At seven months old, she was almost as tall.

25

But her muscles were not yet at adult strength. They tore at her mind in pain and exhaustion.

The two had tailed off to the rear of the fleeing mob, as Beauty's strength began to fail and Bonny stayed alongside her with the instinct of a mother for her daughter.

The quarter horses were only metres behind.

A fallen log lay in their path. Beauty went to clear it, but in her panic and feebleness, her hind legs clipped a small branch and she fell.

In an instant she had regained her feet and her balance, but the pursuers had gained vital ground. Beauty heard their horses' breath. Now they were on her flank.

The roar of a hostile beast was alongside her. A blur passed across her sight. She felt the rope drop over her head and around her neck.

Beauty strained against the pull of the rope. Again she stumbled and then fell once more.

Ahead, as she looked with frightened eyes, she saw her mother, Bonny, pause for a moment, and then, in self-preservation, dash with the others into the shelter and safety of the thick forest.

Beauty could fight no more. The rope tore at her shoulders. She was brought to a halt.

Two snorting horses and two grinning men stood by her.

'Best of the lot,' called Bob to his assistant.

'The younger the better', Jeff shouted back. 'She'll be worth a thousand quid back in town.'

Beauty stood, bowed, but still with gameness in her eyes.

'When we've broken her in and trained her, she'll bring more than that,' replied Bob. 'She's got some good breeding in her. You can see.'

Beauty strained against them, but the men forced a halter on her head. She was at their mercy. In her state of exhaustion, she could offer no resistance.

Then began the slow trek back to where the men had left their truck near the Park boundary.

Beauty's days of freedom were over.

CHAPTER 6

Bob Morrison was a hard man.

His father had brought him up to think of himself first and to suspect everyone else of the worst motives.

'You look after Number One,' he'd say to Bob. 'No-one else will.'

By the time he was grown-up, he regarded the whole world as something to be exploited for his own advantage.

He treated both humans and animals with the same contempt. In the case of the horses he dealt with, his contempt often turned into cruelty.

Bob worked at various jobs in the bush. He felled timber for a logging contractor; he worked in a timber mill when they were short of men; he did some fencing on the farms round about.

As well, he'd buy and sell cattle and horses, and run them on his few acres.

Jeff was one of Bob's cronies. He drifted around town, picking up whatever work he could. At heart he didn't like Bob's way of life, but he had never had good models to follow in his life, so was swayed by the older man's confident manner and aggressive attitude to the world.

Beauty arrived at Bob's farm late in the day.

The truck was backed up to the yards and a ramp put in place. The tailgate of the truck was swung open.

Bob was holding tight to the rope from Beauty's halter. He leaned over and gave the filly several whacks on her rump with a thick stick.

'Out!' he shouted.

Beauty wanted to escape from the blows, but was fearful of the slope of the ramp in front of her. She stalled.

Bob rained down blows on her back.

'Out, you dumb dog!' he screamed. 'You're mine now and you'll do what I tell you!'

Jeff jumped on the back of the truck and pushed Beauty towards the ramp. Beauty lashed out at him with her hind legs. Jeff swore under his breath and belted the horse with his fist.

Dizzy with fear and uncertainty, Beauty at last plunged towards the ramp, which dropped steeply away to the yard beneath. Half sliding, half falling, she hit the earth, and righted herself. Her eyes were ablaze, her nostrils flared, her head held high, ready for flight.

But there would be no flight.

Beauty was barred in by the high rails of the stockyard. Bob held firmly to the rope which restrained her.

Beauty reared again and again, but the rope held firm. The halter around her head tightened with every movement she made.

At last she quietened, for the moment subdued.

Bob tied the young horse to a corner post. 'A short lead,' he said to Jeff. 'Can't hurt herself then. We'll leave her for a while. Give her time to come to terms with herself.'

Jeff laughed.

The two men dusted off their clothing and walked towards the house.

'Not a bad day's work!' Bob snorted.

CHAPTER 7

Molly enjoyed being at High School. In many ways it was similar to the previous year. She continued to travel to school on the same bus, with Charlie, the same bus driver. Most of her Primary School friends were with her at the new school, including her best friend, Prue.

She found it interesting to have several teachers rather than just Mrs O'Brien. And she liked meeting other girls and boys who had been at different primary schools.

But Molly continued to grieve for her lost pony. Beauty was never out of her mind

Months had passed with no sign of the horses. Molly continued to scan the mountain slopes using her father's binoculars. Each time, she put them down disappointed.

Molly, however, was determined not to give in without a fight.

A new idea began to form in her mind. She thought about it for a long time before she dared to speak to her mother.

'If Beauty won't come back to me,' she finally said to Janet one night, 'I'm going to go to her. I'll go and find her … and bring her back,' she added after a pause.

Janet was taken aback with the boldness of Molly's idea.

The idea that anyone could actually go into the high bush country and rescue the two lost horses had never occurred to her. Once within that high hostile country, they were gone for ever, it had seemed to her.

Janet thought about Molly's plan for a long time.

She was sceptical that it could succeed, but because she admired Molly's never-say-die spirit so much she eventually went along with it.

They began to make their plans.

By the end of the week it was settled. As soon as the holidays came, the two of them – mother and daughter - would set off into the National Park in search of the lost horses.

* * *

The Easter holidays were late that year. The cold winds of autumn were a reminder that winter lay ahead. Before long, snow would cover the higher slopes of the National Park.

Doubts began to creep into Molly's mind.

If they did find the mob, would they even be able to get close to them?

Molly thought more deeply about how to go about the task.

If they were ever to get back their horses, she began to realise, they would have to do it gradually. The first stage would be to win the horses' trust, to be allowed to come close to them, even to touch them. Without that there was no chance of success.

'All those horses were once tamed,' Molly argued. 'They were, or their fathers and mothers were. Or their grandparents. It's not as if they were kangaroos or wombats. They must have an instinct of being with humans, even if it's hidden deep in their minds.'

*   *   *

As the time neared, Molly and Janet made their final preparations.

Even Peter, Molly's father, had rung up when he heard about it. Janet had emailed him as a precaution in case she and Molly struck trouble in the bush. 'If you get into any trouble, ring me up, and I'll be there in a flash,' he told Janet.

Janet was doubtful of her husband's good intentions. It was the first time they had been in contact for a long time. But deep down she felt warmed by his message.

Janet worried they would not get a signal on her mobile phone in that isolated country, but she kept that thought to herself.

Despite everything, if on this first attempt they could find the mob and come close to Bonny and Beauty that would be a huge success. 'One thing at a time,' she said to Molly. 'Rome wasn't built in a day,' (and Molly had to look that up on the internet to find out what she meant!)

'Beauty will be big now,' she said to her mother. 'Nearly as big as Bonny.'

There were two men who could have told Janet and Molly that their attempt would be in vain, that Beauty was already a prisoner in their rough hands.

In her ignorance, however, hope continued to grow in Molly's heart.

CHAPTER 8

They set out early on the first Monday of the holidays.

Janet carried a backpack with their tent and sleeping bags. A water bottle hung from the straps. They were confident of re-filling it from the clear water in the gullies higher up in the mountains. In her pack, Molly had their supplies for two days as well as other important items – a torch, fire-lighting material, binoculars, a first-aid kit, and, most precious of all, to Molly's mind, some bread soaked in molasses and a small chunk broken off from a salt lick. 'Beauty won't be able to resist these,' she smiled to her mother.

They found it easy going to begin with. The lower hillsides were covered in scrub, mostly stunted wattle, with patches of rough grass.

'There are good pickings here for the horses,' Janet thought. 'Why haven't we sighted them from the farm?' She said nothing to Molly about that, however. 'Maybe they've had a bad fright, and they're keeping themselves up in the higher country, away from danger,' she mused.

Soon they encountered rougher going. They were in denser bush now – the last belt of tall trees below the winter snow line. There were granite boulders to be got around, and pebbles of small rock to be avoided. No good to roll one's ankle on one of those, thought Molly.

In the afternoon they worked their way around the slope rather than heading straight up. Janet had an idea there was clearer country this way, where the horses might be camped.

They were searching for signs of the mob – hoof prints, or bark rubbed from the tree trunks where the horses might have been scratching themselves.

Late that day, just before they made camp, they came across the first signs of the horses. There, in a marshy area alongside one of the little gully streams, was a tangle of horse prints.

Molly was overjoyed, but her mother pointed out the crusty sides to these tracks.

'It's quite a while since they were here,' she told Molly.

But Molly put that warning aside. That night she slept in the warm hope of catching up with her Beauty the next day.

*   *   *

Mid-morning of the second day, Janet and Molly were working their way around a bluff on the western side of the mountain that towered above them.

They had come across more tracks, fresher this time, they thought.

'Somewhere here,' Molly said to her mother. 'Surely!'

"Well they certainly won't be up there,' Janet added, looking up to the bare upper reaches of the mountain above them. 'Nothing but rock there.'

They would need to begin their return home straight after eating their lunch. They had two hours, at the most, till then, to find the mob, or to admit failure.

*   *   *

Molly saw them first.

The horses stood across a gully, beneath some gums, in deep shade, perhaps two hundred metres away.

Fortunately they were up-wind. The scent of the humans hadn't carried to them.

Janet and Molly stood stock-still. Molly scanned the scene. She had only a few seconds. She strained to make out her beloved filly and the mare, Bonny.

'Can you ...?' she whispered to Janet. 'Can you see them?'

Janet reached for the binoculars ... but it was too late.

The wild horses suddenly caught wind of the intruders, and in a split second they were gone.

With a flash of colour, the beasts plunged into the dense bush country beyond. Molly could hear the sound of their hooves as they raced away.

'It's no good now,' Janet exclaimed. 'They're gone for good.'

Molly squirmed with disappointment.

'Did you see Beauty?' she rasped in a broken voice. 'Did you see her? Or Bonny?'

But Janet had not seen Beauty.

And Bonny? Janet was unsure. There was a snatch of chestnut as the horses wheeled away that could have been Bonny.

But she thought it best not to say that to Molly. The thought of the mare being there without the foal might be too much for her to bear.

'They must have been on the far side,' she said, to comfort her daughter, 'where we couldn't see them.'

As they made their way back to the farm, Janet was mulling the scene over and over in her mind.

Even if Bonny, the mare, was with the mob, why hadn't they seen the foal, Beauty? Had she been injured? Or shot? Or had the brumbies rejected her? Or was she there all the time, with the others? Was it just bad luck they hadn't sighted her?

In her heart of hearts she feared the worst.

But Molly had bounced back from her first disappointment. 'At least we found them,' she said. 'Next time we'll get close, and Beauty will come to me.'

Little did she realise that at that moment, Beauty was standing forlornly in the yard of a stranger not so very far from Molly's own home, and that there her pony's mind dimly turned back to Molly, just as Molly's mind was reaching out to her.

CHAPTER 9

Bob Morrison examined the scar on the point of Beauty's shoulder, the scar she received when she had burst through the barbed wire many weeks earlier. 'A clean cut! Not the sort of wound you'd get in the bush,' he muttered.

What was this young filly's past? he wondered.

He soon dismissed the thought, however. His task now was to begin the breaking-in process, to introduce Beauty to bit and bridle, then perhaps, later, to the saddle.

It was too soon to think of putting a rider on her back. That would have to wait until the horse was fully grown.

He was, after all, an experienced horseman. He knew that to put weight on a young horse before the knees were fully formed might cripple her later in life – and he had his mind set on selling this horse in perfect condition as a riding horse to a discerning buyer.

It was enough for the present for the filly to be socialised into human company, to learn acceptance to human mastery, and to be taught to follow quietly where she was led.

Bob had allowed the filly to stand alone in the yard for several days. She had a rough nylon halter on her head fixed by a rope tied to the corner of the railings. She was given feed and water, but there was no company. Bob kept his other horses in a far paddock. Never in her short life had Beauty been quite, quite, alone.

Now, as the man untied the leading-rope, his accomplice, Jeff, arrived. He spun his utility alongside the yard with a spray of dirt, jumped out, slammed the door, and shouted a greeting to his partner.

'Quit the noise, willya!' the older man called, throwing a surly look across the rails. 'Do you want to scare the hell out of this thing?'

Beauty was indeed scared. Her body tensed. Her eyes were intent on the man with the rope, but her senses took in everything around her. They spelt nothing but danger and fear.

Bob pulled on the rope, gently at first, then with increasing force.

Beauty dug her heels in.

He came alongside her and shoved forward against her shoulder.

Beauty spun her head around and bit at him.

The man shouted a curse, and slapped the free end of the rope across her flank.

Beauty shied away from him.

Again, Bob tried to move the horse forward by pulling on the rope. He was aware of the young man watching him. 'Can't let him see this thing beat me,' he thought.

Bob pulled on the lead. He lashed Beauty again and again with the end of the rope. He picked up a stick and beat her with it. He swore at her.

Still Beauty would not move.

In the end, Jeff climbed over the rails. He took a stick and beat Beauty around the flanks and thighs.

Bob tugged on the rope until Beauty's neck felt torn in two.

The strength of the men and the pain eventually told. Beauty could stand no more.

Unwillingly she prodded a few steps forward.

Throughout the morning the process went on and on.

The men pulled and pushed and belted the young filly until she would stagger forward.

By lunchtime, the men were satisfied. Beauty had buckled under their persistence and bullying. She followed Bob's lead warily, unwillingly.

He tied her once more to the railings, and the two men walked away.

'Not a bad morning's work,' grinned Bob.

'I've heard that before,' laughed Jeff.

They went into the house, leaving Beauty once more alone.

* * *

The winter months ticked by.

Cold winds swept over the foothills. Snow covered the high peaks, and dustings of light snow fell around Molly's farm and on the farm of Bob Morrison in the next valley, some twenty kilometres away.

A second attempt by Molly to reach the wild horses was impossible in these conditions. Until the spring, at any rate.

Beauty's training continued.

Her coat was thickening to ward off the winter weather, and she continued to grow towards her full height.

On the days when Morrison was at work, Beauty stood alone in her yard.

On the other days, she would be given more training, mostly, by Bob alone. Sometimes Jeff came to help.

Reluctantly, Beauty allowed herself to be led out of the yard and around the outside paddock.

43

When Bob ran with her, she trotted unwillingly after him.

When she refused, or pulled against his leading, he gave her a blow across her rump with the stick he kept handy.

In time, Beauty learnt to turn to the left when Bob pulled her in that direction, and to the right when he pulled the rope the other way. And to stop when he jerked suddenly on the rope. When he pulled her from the back, Beauty was forced to stumble awkwardly backwards.

All this time, Beauty had just a rope halter on her head. Now Bob decided it was time for her to have a bit and bridle.

Beauty was tied with a short lead against a corner-post, and then squashed against the railing by the weight of Bob's body leaning against her. Jeff leaned against her hindquarters.

Beauty felt trapped, but then the worst of it began.

Bob slipped off the halter from the filly's head and passed the crown of the bridle loosely over her ears. The feel of the metal bridle frightened the young horse. Each time Bob's hands passed across her face, Beauty pulled away. Each time, Jeff gave her a cut with a stick.

Bob put a finger to the side of Beauty's mouth and pushed into her back teeth.

The filly didn't know what she was expected to do, and shook her head vigorously up and down.

Bob was unusually patient. He'd done this many times before.

He rubbed the horse's gums. Beauty began to relax her mouth and in an instant, Bob had slipped the bit between her teeth, making sure it was over her tongue and not under it. In the same action he pushed the bridle firmly over her head.

Beauty spat at the horrid thing in her mouth. She jerked her head as if trying to spit it out.

All to no avail. The bridle held it firm. As Jeff continued to push against her, Bob secured the straps of the bridle. He buckled down the noseband and throatlatch.

Beauty felt she would choke; the leather seemed to crush her face; the buckles bit into her soft flesh. She had given up all resistance.

'What next?' Jeff asked.

'We'll leave it on till tomorrow, then we'll take it off and put it on again She'll get used to it,' Bob shrugged. 'She'll *have* to!

'And then?'

'Then we get her to mix with the other horses.'

'Kindergarten training,' Jeff smirked. 'And after that?'

'Then we cash in on her. When the weather warms up, those kids will be coming up to old Lombardo's, wanting to do their pony trekking. He'll buy her. I'd bet on it. She'll be good for that thousand quid you spoke about.'

Joe Lombardo ran a pony stables not far from Bob Morrison's farm.

'He can take this one along on one of his pony treks,' added Bob.

'You're a cunning beggar,' said the young man. 'You've got it all worked out.'

'Yeah, I reckon I've got it all worked out,' Bob said.

The two men strolled casually away.

CHAPTER 10

The Peter Pan Riding Stables were three kilometres from Bob Morrison's farm.

Joe and Maria Lombardo were the owners. Joe and Maria had come to Australia from Italy many years earlier. Joe had worked as a leading stable hand and strapper in a big racing stable in the City.

They both had a love of horses. Now, in their older years, they had settled here in the High Country and started up their riding stables.

They named the place after a famous racehorse of the 1930s.

Peter Pan won the Melbourne Cup twice, as well as most of the big races in Melbourne and Sydney.

The Lombardos ran ten or twelve horses in their stables. Every now and then, they'd sell one to a private buyer and buy in a suitable replacement.

At the weekends and especially in the school holidays children from the bigger towns round about and also from the City would come to Joe and Maria to learn horse-riding and how to care for horses.

Even Molly herself, when she was younger, had spent a weekend at the Peter Pan Stables, and her friend, Prue, also had come here. The Lombardos were careful and considerate teachers.

In the school holidays, the children could take part in pony treks. Half a dozen ponies would be ridden along the quiet country roads over two or three days.

At night, the trekkers would stay at special places where camping was allowed.

Sometimes these treks would be in the National Park.

Before each of these treks, the Lombardos would get the necessary permit from the Park authorities. They would take the horses by horse float to the entrance to the Park, where the riders and leaders would join them, and the trek would begin.

The trek leaders were local men and women chosen by Joe and Maria. They themselves stayed back to look after the rest of the horses.

Bob Morrison was one of the people employed by Joe and Maria Lombardo to lead the pony treks. He would have two others with him, often a husband and wife from the local area.

Before the September holidays came around, Bob drove over to the Riding Stables.

'I've got a young filly at my place,' he told Joe. 'Should turn out to be a good one for your team here.'

Joe and Maria showed interest. They'd bought another horse from Morrison some years earlier.

'She's well-bred,' Bob went on. 'And I've got her trained to bit and bridle.'

'How old?' asked Joe.

'Just a yearling,' replied Bob. 'Too young to be ridden yet'.

Joe glanced at his wife. She nodded her head. It was good to have young horses coming into their team.

'All right,' said Joe. 'Bring her over, and if I like the look of her, I'll take her. We'll talk about a price when I see her.'

Jeff was waiting when Bob returned home.

'All hunky-dory,' said Bob as he climbed down from his truck. He spoke confidently. 'They'll have her,' he said. 'You can bet your boots.'

They didn't spare a glance at Beauty as she stood watching them from the stockyard.

To Molly, Beauty had been a precious friend, cared for and loved. To these two, she was just another animal, whose value was to be measured in dollars and cents.

'We'll get our thousand for her, don't you worry,' said Bob. 'If we don't, we'll find some other place to get rid of her.'

As if she understood these words, Beauty looked up to the mountains that rose high above her.

A flicker of remembrance crossed her mind. She shook her mane and stared down into the ground.

CHAPTER 11

Two days later, the move was made.

Beauty was loaded into the back of Bob's truck. The truck was backed up to the loading ramp, and Beauty was pushed and prodded up the slope. Jeff shouted at her from behind. The way he saw it, if you frightened a horse, it would do what you wanted. He couldn't understand that a horse loves to be treated kindly and will do what is wanted out of its good nature if handled that way.

Going down the ramp at the end of the short journey was worse.

No horse likes to have a slope falling away in front of it, but with Bob pulling and Jeff pushing and shouting, Beauty finally tumbled down onto the firm ground beneath.

She shook her mane proudly, as if to maintain some dignity in the face of the way these two men were treating her.

Joe and Maria studied the newcomer carefully.

'Never buy a pig in a poke,' Joe said, smiling.

'Just buy a horse from a bloke,' Bob replied, and roared with laughter at his wit.

Joe walked around the filly. He felt her fetlocks and examined her knees. He gently persuaded her to open her mouth so he could look at her teeth. All this Beauty accepted quietly. There was something about this man that gave her confidence. Joe stroked her forehead.

Maria gave her husband a glance of approval.

'Seems all right,' said Joe, finally. 'How much were you thinking?'

There was some discussion between the two men. Eventually it was decided that Bob would get his price. Joe wrote out a cheque, and Bob wrote a receipt on a piece of paper he found in his pocket.

Beauty, like an orphan from a foundling hospital, had found a new home.

She watched as Bob's truck drove out of the yard.

'Will I ever see you again?' she thought.

*   *   *

There were twelve other horses at the stables at that time.

Joe Lombardo knew it was sometimes difficult for a new horse to be put in with others.

For the first three days, he let Beauty into a small paddock next to the others. Beauty became used to their strange smell. She could tell that some of them were friendlier to her than others.

One pony in particular – a colt a little older and bigger than Beauty – came to her and rubbed necks across the rails. But one of the others, a much older mare, who seemed to be the leader, kept her distance. She snorted and pawed the ground when the others sniffed at Beauty.

Each day, Joe and Maria moved among the horses. They led them into the stables where they were checked over carefully and lightly groomed. Their early spring coats shone with health and good care.

Meanwhile, Beauty was left in her yard. Joe came to her several times each day and gently spoke to her. He moved slowly, keeping himself where Beauty could see him clearly. After a little while, he came alongside her and quietly stroked her shoulders, murmuring softly while he did so.

By the third day, Beauty would come towards Joe when he came into the yard. He'd have a piece of carrot or apple, which Beauty would take from his hand. Joe would rub his knuckles over her, speaking soothing words.

For Beauty, it was a return to the time of her first months of life when a girl she dimly remembered would caress her and give her treats to eat. Beauty's confidence in humans was gradually being restored by Joe's kind management.

On the fourth day, Joe decided it was time for Beauty to be given a good grooming. He took her by the halter rope into the stable yard itself. Quietly, he eased her into one of the stalls, and tied her with cross ties to the two sides of the stall.

Joe looked carefully at Beauty's coat. It was shaking off its winter roughness, but showed all the signs of neglect.

Joe began work. Beginning on the horse's near side, as he stroked her with his left hand, he used the curry comb to loosen the dirt on her sides, then finished off with the body brush.

Beauty stood still. Joe was a friend, she knew, not one to be feared. She began to enjoy the circular strokes of the brushes and pushed her head against Joe when he stroked her forehead.

Joe moved to the off side. Carefully, he worked on Beauty's hips and legs, then began to comb out her mane, then her tail He clipped away some of the straggling strands of hair.

Finally, he examined Beauty's hooves. No problems there. There had been no hard ground for Beauty.

Joe called Maria from the house.

'Look at our new beauty,' he said proudly.

Maria looked with wonder at the transformation that had taken place.

'A beauty all right,' she said. 'Where did she get that colour from? I've never seen such a beautiful chestnut.'

'She needs a name,' said Joe.

'I think you just named her,' Maria smiled back.

'Just named her? How do you mean?'

'What did you say just then? – "Look at our new beauty". Isn't that a good name?'

And that is how this filly came by her second name - 'New Beauty'.

* * *

On the following day, Joe moved his New Beauty in with the other horses.

He stayed with her for a short time before moving out of the yard. He continued to watch as the horses intermingled.

The other horses were giving Beauty a suspicious but not unfriendly inspection at close quarters. Only one of them kept away, Joe noticed – the old mare, Domino. Domino was called by that name because she was black with white splashes.

'I'll have to watch her,' Joe said to himself, as he walked away.

* * *

The mare drove Beauty savagely against the railings.

She was a big and heavy horse and had the strength that comes with greater age. She bent low and shouldered Beauty against a corner post. Beauty felt the pain of the impact. The older horse held her there while her teeth sank into Beauty's neck.

Beauty squealed in terror. Struggling violently, she managed to free herself.

The mare swung round to the other horses. She rounded them into a corner, enforcing her authority over them.

Beauty was left alone, licking her wounds.

It seemed that she had escaped the horror of life at Bob Morrison's farm only to suffer the tyranny of one of her own kind.

In the evening, Joe and Maria came out to settle the horses down for the night. They noticed Beauty standing alone.

'Hope that mare hasn't been bullying her,' Joe commented to his wife. 'I've been worried about that.'

'We'll check them again in an hour or two,' Maria replied.

When the couple came out some time later, they were pleased to see one of the others standing alongside the newcomer.

It was the one they called Frosty, a pale grey colt, a two-year-old, born in the spring a year before Beauty herself.

The two horses stood side by side. Frosty's neck lay against Beauty's.

Maria smiled in the gathering darkness. 'At least New Beauty's got one friend,' she said as she took her husband's arm.

They walked back together towards their home.

CHAPTER 12

As the months of winter wore on, Molly's enthusiasm began to wane.

The excitement of having found the mob the previous Easter holidays had become a distant memory. A mood of deep melancholy took hold of her.

Her thoughts constantly travelled to the bushland in the National Park nearby.

In her imagination, Beauty's mob of wild horses would come sweeping through the bushland, across the open spaces, from gully to gully, past giant boulders and marshlands. In her mind, they were always on the move, always galloping, always in the distance, just as in the fleeting glimpse she had of them on that day of drama and disappointment.

Molly was totally unaware of what had happened to Beauty. In her dreaming, Beauty still ran free in the bushland of the National Park. In reality, Beauty had been taken captive, mistreated, broken and beaten, and although she had come through to a better place, still suffered from the attacks of one of her own kind.

As the weeks of dreariness passed by, however, another bold idea began to take shape in Molly's mind.

It had seemed impossible to begin with. How could she, a young girl, in an isolated country place, bring a plan such as this to fulfilment?

And, at any rate, how could it help her regain her precious horse?

Despite her doubts, Molly persevered. In her probing mind, a new thought emerged.

Her mind became fixed on her father, Peter. Could it be that he could help her in her quest to recover her precious pony? It was a very long time since she had seen him, but she knew he thought of her. Hadn't he offered to help her and her mother in their attempt to find Beauty last Easter?

With her father, perhaps, lay the key to getting Beauty back with her once again.

One evening she spoke of her idea with her mother. She was nervous, not just because Janet might pooh-pooh the idea, but also because she did not know whether her mother would like to talk about Peter.

'Dad is still working down at the coast, isn't he?' she began, cautiously.

Janet wondered what was coming. 'Yes, still down there'.

'And he works on the oil rigs?'

'Still there,' replied Janet.

'He's got a pilot's licence, hasn't he?'

'I know he used to have. Why, what's on your mind?'

'You're going to think this is silly,' Molly went on. She paused. Janet waited for her to proceed.

'I want him to help us get Beauty back.'

All Molly's ideas now tumbled out. 'If we got an aeroplane – you know, one of those little ones – and Dad flew it, I could go with him, and we could fly over the Park and find the horses. Then we'd know where they were and we'd know where to go and look for them and this time I know I'd get Beauty to come back with me.' Molly finished with a rush.

Janet took some time to reply. She couldn't see how all this would help recover the horses, but at least bringing Peter into the attempt would open a new angle. And it might help to bring Molly out of her doldrums.

She thought carefully before she spoke. 'I think it's a good idea,' she said at last. 'But there are a lot of things that could go wrong with it.'

Molly waited eagerly for her mother to go on.

'First we don't know if your father still has his pilot's licence. And we'd have to find someone with a plane who lives not far away, and they'd have to agree for your father to use it. And it would cost a lot of money to hire the plane.'

Molly had thought of all these problems, but to her mind, they could all be overcome. She remained silent, however. It seemed her mother wanted to go on.

It was a while before Janet spoke again. 'Of course …' she began. She paused. What she had in her mind was difficult to say. 'Molly, we may be able to get a plane. Your father may come and fly it. We may find the horses. But then …'

Janet took a long breath. 'You see, I'm not sure about the last bit. We still have to get Beauty and Bonny back, even if we know where they are. They've been with the brumbies for a long time now. They mightn't want to come back.' Janet paused again. 'That's the hard part, getting them to come back with you.'

It was a thought that Molly had had before, but she kept pushing it away. She did the same now. 'Oh Mummy,' she burst out. 'They'll come! I know they'll come! I just know it!'

Janet looked across at her daughter where she sat at the kitchen table. Her face was glowing with hope and anticipation, but Janet thought she could read in her daughter's eyes the doubts she herself held. Could she bridge the gap between Molly's youthful yearnings and the practical difficulties that lay in her path?

'Very well,' she said, after a time. 'The first thing is to ring your father and talk it through with him.'

She went on, 'Don't be disappointed if it all comes to nothing, Molly. It's a long chance we'll be taking.'

The two of them sat in silence for some time.

* * *

Beauty's first birthday was in the middle of August.

Molly lit a candle for her and placed it on the dinner table. She propped a baby photo of the horse alongside it.

It was on that same evening that Molly rang her father.

Despite Peter's neglect of his family, he thought of Janet and Molly every day. It wasn't through a lack of love for them that he stayed away. He couldn't really explain why. It was more his own shame and sense of guilt that kept him from being with them ... and he wondered if Janet would want him back after all the years he had neglected her.

Peter was surprised – and delighted - to get Molly's call. It was early evening, after he had finished work for the day.

They talked of many things before Molly told him the reason for her call. They spoke of Molly's coming birthday and of her new school, of the farm and of the wintry weather.

'Beauty is a year old today,' Molly said at last. Peter had heard from Janet of their failure to get to the wild horses and bring the two home, Bonny and Beauty. He felt that Molly was leading up to something so he waited for her to go on.

'I've got a plan, Dad,' she went on, and explained to her father her idea about the aeroplane. Peter listened to what Molly had to say. He was amazed that his daughter could think up such a bold scheme, though he too was very doubtful whether it would help in the long run. He kept silent about his doubts, however, and spoke encouragingly to his daughter.

'I'll see what I can do,' he said. 'I've got some holiday time due to me. I'll try to arrange something.' Molly had already suggested the coming school holidays for the venture.

'And I'll have to brush up on my flying,' he added with a laugh. 'I'll get one of the men down here to take me up with them.' Peter's company had several light planes they used in their off-shore work with the oil rigs.

'And I'll work out where I can get a plane up in your part of the world. Shouldn't be too hard. Some of those big farms have planes they use.' He had another thought. 'Maybe I'll ring one or two of the airfields up your way. They may have a plane we can hire. Or they might tell us where we can get one.'

After he put the phone down, Peter worried that he had been too encouraging to his daughter. So much could go wrong with this plan, would it have been better to discourage her from the whole project?

His instincts told him, however, that Molly needed support. What other girl of her age could have come up with such an idea?

Besides, he was pleased with the prospect of seeing his daughter … and Janet as well. Could this be the beginning of the end of his long isolation?

CHAPTER 13

The fact that Beauty had made a pal in the colt Frosty didn't mean the end of the mare, Domino's, bullying.

Now she began to attack both Beauty and Frosty, though Beauty was her special target. In the wild, behaviour like this would probably result in the two younger horses leaving the herd and trying to attach themselves to another mob. But here in captivity there was no escape.

The mare was cunning enough not to attack when Maria or Joe were nearby. In their absence, however, she would drive them into a corner, rush them against the railings, and bite and kick them. She isolated them by keeping the other horses away from them.

Under this treatment, Beauty began to lose weight. Her coat, still rough from the winter, remained daggy. Joe noticed her condition. 'That filly isn't picking up like she should,' he said to Maria. Again he suspected the old mare of mistreating her. He looked across to the mare, but she was standing demurely in a far corner. Still, Joe knew the ways of horses. His brow furrowed. 'One thing for certain,' he added. 'They can't both go on the trek on Saturday.'

*   *   *

The September school holidays had come, and half a dozen children were gathered at the Peter Pan Riding Stables to begin their pony trek into the National Park.

Maria had received the Park permit. Joe had organised the three trek leaders. First, there was a married couple, Frank Simmons and his wife, Mai. Mai had come to Australia as a child with her family when they fled Vietnam as refugees. When she grew up, Mai moved to the country and had fallen in love with horses. Both Frank and Mai were experienced in the bush, and had taken treks for Joe and Maria before. The third leader was Bob Morrison. The three leaders would bring their own mounts.

The trek was due to begin on the second Wednesday of the school holidays and would last for three days. The group would return on Friday afternoon. The children would then have the weekend at home before going back to school.

Joe spoke to the young riders at his stables before they set out. He reminded them of the need for safety, and of being alert to the dangers of the bush. He told them of the importance of doing what the trek leaders told them to do. Finally, he urged them to look after each other, especially the younger ones. The parents stood at the rear and listened in as well.

Joe liked to do things very formally. He called the riders forward, one by one.

'Skye,' he called, and a thirteen-year-old girl came to the front. 'Your pony is Comrade,' and he pointed out a bay gelding standing nearby.

'Trent,' he called next, and a boy of eleven came forward. 'Your pony is Prince,' and again he pointed out Trent's horse.

So it went on. The other four came out – Claire, Zoe, Calvin, and Charley. Each was given their horse.

In fact, this was mostly for show. The children had each ridden their allotted horse on previous occasions while attending the stables.

But Joe wasn't finished. 'Two other horses will be on the trek,' he announced. 'Frosty over there,' and here he pointed out the two-year-old, Beauty's friend. 'Frosty will be the pack-horse. He will carry your bedding and provisions.'

He pointed out another horse, a younger filly. 'And this one,' Joe went on, 'she will be going as part of her training. Her name is New Beauty. Frosty and New Beauty will be led throughout the trek by Frank and Mia.'

On this occasion, Joe had more to say to the young riders.

'Think of your horse always,' he began. 'Remember what a privilege it is to ride on such a wonderful creature. For thousands of years horses and humans have placed their trust in each other. Today you become part of that long

67

history. In his way, your horse is more intelligent than you are. Listen to the signals he sends to you. It is not so much that you are to ride your horse on this trek, but that you and he are to travel together.'

Joe's eloquence had run out and he turned to practical matters. 'Now, Maria and I will start loading the horses on to my truck. You riders will go with your parents to the starting point at the entrance to the National Park.

'We meet there in one hour,' he concluded. 'Good riding to you all.'

CHAPTER 14

The little band of adventurers made their way along the bush trail.

If someone could have looked down on them from above, they would have seemed like a row of ants, stretched out in line, Bob Morrison in front, the six children following, with Mia and Frank bringing up the rear, except that, tagging along behind, led by ropes, came Frosty and Beauty.

Frosty carried the children's gear in two saddle bags, weighted equally on either side. Beauty, who had not yet been trained to the saddle, was alongside her horse-pal, untroubled by bit or bridle. She had a halter round her head and a long leading rope attached. It was part of Joe's plan that Beauty would benefit from the experience of being part of the team of horses.

The children rode side by side where the track allowed it; in other places they went in single file.

By lunchtime on the first day they had covered some six or seven kilometres and Bob called a halt alongside a mountain spring. Each child had brought sandwiches for this meal, so they were soon on the march again.

By four in the afternoon they reached the official camp-site. Frank and Mia organised the setting up of the tents with the help of the children, and then the evening meal.

Bob Morrison considered this sort of thing quite beneath his dignity. He did help the children with the 'horsey' things – taking off the saddles and bridles, replacing them on each horse with a halter. Then they fed and watered the animals and tied them up to the highlines Bob had set up near the camp.

There were three of these highlines, each one tied between two trees, with the horses individually tied to it.

There were no other riding parties in camp, and the children had an early night. It had been an uneventful day.

Perhaps tomorrow would be different!

* * *

The trail led up to higher ground. By mid-morning, the children were bracing themselves against the cold. The wind swung to the west and carried cold air from the snow high above them. The smell of the bush was strong.

Mia was worried about the filly she was leading – the yearling who'd come along for training. Beauty had become nervous. She frisked at sudden movements. She

70

pulled on the lead rope. She swung her head high and wide.

Mia called to Bob Morrison, 'You might have to help me here,' she yelled. Bob was in his usual place at the front of the riders. He waited for Mia at the tail to catch up to him.

Bob watched the antics of the pony. He knew all about this one, of course. He knew all about Beauty's past. It was not so very far from here that he himself had chased after her and caught her. Not far away that he had loaded her on to his truck and carted her away. Not that he was ever going to say anything about that to anybody!

Bob immediately understood what was going on.

Beauty was back amongst the places of her past. Her body stirred as half-forgotten memories of the old days surged through her. As a young pony she had trodden these very tracks. Here she had run free with her mother and the brumby mob after she had broken out from the farm.

This was why Beauty was so unsettled.

There was something else, Bob realised.

The change of wind had brought the scent of the wild bush horses. Bob glanced away to the westward. 'They'll be there,' he muttered under his breath. 'They'll be watching us.'

But to Mia he said nothing about this. 'Keep a firm hold on her,' he said. 'She'll settle down. I'll stay behind you.'

But Beauty's skittishness was only increased by Bob's nearness. She continued to jerk and lunge sideways. Here was the man who had treated her so cruelly, this man, near her, alongside her, behind her. Beauty's eyes were staring wide, her nostrils flared.

Sensing that Beauty was reacting to his presence, Bob thought it wise to move away. He resumed his place at the head of the party.

*   *   *

At about eleven o'clock, the trekking group was making its way around the gradient of a clear hillside.

The wind had dropped to a gentle breeze and the sky was clear.

The riders heard a low drone in the distance. It seemed out of place in this remote spot.

A small plane cleared the horizon on the riders' left hand side. The drone became the sharp buzz of an angry bee. The plane was quite low – just a hundred metres from the ground.

It was coming from the south, straight towards them, headed for the high country farther on. The horses were startled and shuffled nervously. The children craned their necks to make out what was going on.

The plane roared overhead, then banked and rose as it neared the high ground. In a moment it had swung out of sight.

Beauty was the one horse to become agitated. She tossed her head violently and frisked sideways. Her reaction affected Frosty as well. Frank and Mia had their hands full to control them.

The coming of the plane was a small wonder to the children. It set off a chorus of chatter. 'Could you see who was in it?' Calvin called. 'Do you think it was going to crash?' asked Charley, the youngest rider. 'Do you think it was somebody who knew us?' Trent sang out. All questions, but there were no answers.

And then, it came again. The plane, now higher in the air, came from in front of them and circled in a wide arc, only to disappear above the high slopes to their right.

Three times the plane circled above them as the trekkers watched.

'There's something going on,' Frank called to Bob. 'Somebody lost, do you think?'

'Wouldn't think so,' he replied. 'It's a private plane, not an SES one or the Police. Probably just a joy-ride.'

The plane continued to circle, but now farther to the west. On each circuit it swung perilously close to the ground. Eventually it disappeared from view.

None the wiser, the trekking party moved on towards their destination, the Park entrance, where the parents would be waiting, and also Joe and Maria with the truck.

CHAPTER 15

Molly's father, Peter, had been true to his word.

The day after Molly's phone call he had gone online to find a list of country airfields. Wondarup, he discovered, was the closest, some forty kilometres from the farm.

He rang immediately. 'Yes,' the Club manager had told him. 'I could arrange a plane for you. It's a private one. One of our members owns it, but he hires it out to others now and then.'

Peter wanted to know what type of plane it was. 'It's a Cessna 152. Two-seater. You'll need to have had 100 hours flying time.'

As an afterthought, Peter asked about the landing strip. 'It's only a grass strip. You all right with that?' came the reply.

Peter showed interest. He had his 100 hours up. He had used grass strips in his younger flying days.

'Of course, you'd have to have your unrestricted pilot's licence and your insurance,' the man went on. 'There are no landing fees, but you'd have to do a couple of circuit checks to start with. And the money.'

He mentioned how much it would cost. Peter whistled between his teeth. 'That's half a week's wages each hour,' he mumbled to himself, then quickly added in his mind, 'but it's worth it for Molly's sake.'

By the end of the day, Peter had arranged a suitable date with Molly – Friday, the last day of the school holidays – and arranged to have the day off for himself. He rang back to the airfield to confirm the booking.

The following weekend Peter went up with one of his friends in one of the Company's planes. He surprised himself with how quickly he rediscovered his flying skills. Besides, he was familiar with the Cessna 152. He had flown one in the old days.

All was in readiness.

*   *   *

The day was fine and visibility was good.

The plane swooped low over the farm. Janet was away at work, but she had left pegged to the ground a double-bed sheet with the large letters 'M' and 'P' pinned to it.

Molly grinned. For a moment her mind was taken off the reason for their flight. She sat back delighting in being in the air and being with her father.

Molly could see clearly the road into the farm, the house and sheds, the steers in their paddock, and the boundary fence between the farm and the National Park.

The cockpit seats were arranged side by side. Peter's voice brought her back to the task in hand. 'We'll assume the horses are on this side of the range,' he called out. 'If they've gone over to the north side of the snow country – over the tops - we'll never get them. But I don't think so. This is their patch, down here. Start looking!' he called.

Peter dipped the plane lower as Molly's eyes strained, searching the country below.

'We'll take it in three bites,' Peter called. 'Three zones. We'll circle over each area two or three times.'

'Till we find them!' Molly shouted back.

'Look there!' she called suddenly. For a moment her heart leapt. Down below were horses. But not the ones she was looking for. Below them was spread out a crocodile-line of horses and riders.

'They'll be from the riding stables. The Peter Pan,' she sang out. 'They do these pony treks in the holidays. I've heard about them. Prue did one once.'

The horses had been pulled up. One or two of the children waved to them. There were two riderless horses at the back of the line, Molly noticed – a grey and a dark-coloured horse. But they looked like miniatures from her height and they were gone so quickly she could make out nothing further.

'I wonder why those two are at the back,' she thought to herself, but in a moment they were gone, and it passed from Molly's mind.

*   *   *

All Peter's skills were now put to the test.

He was over unfamiliar country. The land rose irregularly before him. He had to keep well clear of the higher ground, yet fly low into the valleys, as that is where the horses would most likely be. He had to watch the rise and fall of the land, and at the same time keep watch for signs of the horses, all the while keeping his eye on the controls.

'I'm relying on you,' he called to Molly over the noise of the engine. 'You're Observer Number One!'

Molly took up the binoculars, but soon put them aside. It was bumpy inside the plane, and too hard to focus on the ground beneath. 'Better without the technology,' she muttered.

Ten minutes later, Peter had almost completed the second of his series of circuits. He had already been round twice.

There was no sign of the horses. 'We'll give it one more try,' he called to Molly. 'Then on to the last of our zones.'

Down, down into the valley he swooped, lower than ever before. Molly glanced out to the ground on either side. The rocky hillsides was level with the plane. The tree tops were only metres below, it seemed. Molly felt a terrible tightening in her throat, but she brushed it aside and riveted her eyes on the bush below.

There! On the right! Under the trees! By those boulders! A splash of colour! Sudden movement! Horses rearing! Horses fleeing!

Molly shrieked. 'Dad!' she cried. There was no time even to point. But Peter had seen them too. In one split second he had glimpsed them at the very edge of his vision.

The plane's nose jerked upwards as Peter pulled hard on the controls. The bush fell away giddily beneath, and there was a chance to talk.

'How many?' Peter shouted.

'I don't know,' Molly shouted back. 'Six or seven, I think. Maybe eight.'

'And Beauty?'

There was no reply.

'Beauty? And Bonny?' Peter shouted again.

'I couldn't tell,' Molly rasped, her voice husky with emotion 'I couldn't tell. Go round again!'

Peter did go round again. Twice more he dropped the plane into the valley. Twice more Molly's eyes almost fell from their sockets as she strained to see below.

But the horses had vanished from sight.

Peter took the plane higher. He circled the area three more times. But to no avail.

'They've gone for the tree cover,' he called. 'That's the last we'll see of them.'

'But we found them!' Molly bawled. 'We found them! We know where they are!'

At home that night Molly nestled close to her mother. 'I couldn't tell if Beauty was there,' she said. But she must have been, mustn't she?'

'Yes, Molly, She must have been,' replied Janet.

'And now we know just where to go to find her,' Molly went on.

'Yes, Molly. We do.'

'And bring her back.'

'Yes, Molly, to bring her back.'

CHAPTER 16

The mob had had several disturbances in past months.

There had been the shootings to begin with, then the arrival of the two new horses, and lastly the unnerving experience of the low-flying aeroplane.

After this latest one, they remained unsettled for many days.

The Boss was the worst. He wanted to get back to the higher country, away from this place of danger. He snorted and wrestled with the mare, Queenie.

But it was Queenie who made the decisions. She was wiser. She knew that her charges needed to stay put, to recover their balance, to remain in this valley they knew so well.

The mob was here because of the sweet spring grass that grew in the open areas. They would be here for months, fattening and strengthening themselves for the harsh rigours of winter.

There was another reason for staying put. The new foal had been born only weeks earlier. He needed time to strengthen his tender muscles. And Queenie herself needed the good grass she had here in order to provide milk for her young colt.

For several days after the aeroplane incident, the horses went off their feed. Gradually, however, they resumed their regular pattern of behaviour. They would spend the days grazing the shoots of grass that grew haphazardly in the clearer spaces or nibbling the fresh tips of the shrubs.

There was good water in the streams and cover from the night winds in the lower reaches.

The older of the two fillies, Pretty, was newly in foal, and kept mostly to herself, while Shaggy, whose mother had been lost in the shooting, stayed close to the others.

The two young stallions, Scar and Son of Boss, continued to bother away at each other. Scar showed every sign of discontent. He grazed alone, and continually sniffed the wind for traces of horses running in other mobs. Before next winter he would be gone to seek the company of other horses and other females. He would go of his own accord or The Boss would drive him away.

Meanwhile, the newcomer ran freely with the rest - the deep chestnut mare, whose domestic name had been Bonny, the one who had lost her foal to the horsemen in the terrifying chase many months earlier.

Bonny was also in foal to The Boss, though it would be almost eleven months before her foal would be born.

The horses were not the only occupants of the Park. At night the lumbering wombats left their holes to fossick for food. Wallabies would pass through the horses' camp. The lonely cry of the dingo would disturb them, especially Bonny, who was less used to the bush than the others. In the early morning the chorus of the white-backed magpie roused the animals, and the kookaburras' laughter sent the day to rest. Then the owls would appear. The hoot of the boobook sounded eerily throughout the night.

Bonny took all this in. She was fast becoming a creature of the wild herself.

CHAPTER 17

With the holidays and the pony trek over, the usual pattern was resumed at the Peter Pan Riding Stables.

Children came at weekends for training. They went for short rides around the property and on local roads.

Joe and Maria had their hands full. Bob Harrison came to help, and even Jeff was drafted in when they needed someone extra.

During the week things were quieter. Joe decided it was time for New Beauty, as he called her, to be trained to the saddle.

One morning, he separated the filly from the others, but put her in a yard alongside them. Joe wanted to make her feel as relaxed as possible.

Maria was there, too. Gently, she slipped the bit into Beauty's mouth and took the bridle over her head. With each movement, she gave the horse a bite of carrot and murmured softly in her ear. The straps of the bridle were tied down.

Now for the saddle. Beauty had often seen the others saddled up and with riders on their backs. That had been part of her training.

But despite their best efforts Beauty would not co-operate.

Maria stroked her and spoke softly to her. But as soon as she tried to slip even a saddle cloth over her back, Beauty shied away. Joe came in to try his hand. Beauty continued to back away. She threw her front hooves into the air and shook her head.

The trainers didn't want to force the issue, so left the horse alone for some time.

'I've an idea,' said Maria. 'She needs a mate in there with her.'

Joe had seen this done before. 'Frosty,' he said immediately. 'He's her best mate. They're together all the time.'

Frosty was brought into the yard with Beauty. As Beauty watched, he was saddled, standing quietly all the while.

Now Maria tried again with Beauty, using kind words and soft stroking. This time Beauty let first the saddle cloth, then the saddle, be placed on her back. At every step she was given another piece of her favourite carrot.

Now, gingerly, Maria reached under the horse and took the girth strap, fed it beneath the horse, and buckled it loosely in place.

Now Beauty was led round and round the yard on a long lead – an exercise she was well used to – before being left alone with Frosty for the rest of the morning.

Beauty, with Frosty's companionship, settled down once again.

In the afternoon, Maria was able to slip into the saddle. First, she placed a portable step alongside the pony, pressed firmly on her back until all signs of nervousness were gone, and then eased herself into the saddle. At the same time, Joe reassured the horse from in front, giving her treats, partly as a reward for her good behaviour and partly to distract her attention.

Maria dismounted and remounted several times. By the end of the afternoon, Beauty was walking round the yard with Maria on board. Frosty remained in close attendance. Beauty still had to learn to accept directions from the reins – how to turn to left and right, and to pull up when commanded.

But that could wait for another day.

*   *   *

The old mare continued to mistreat Beauty.

As the weather warmed, the horses spent more time in the paddock rather than in the stables themselves.

Here, more distant from the supervision of Joe and Maria, the mare would continue her bullying. On one occasion, she bit Beauty on the neck. It caused the blood to flow freely as it had on the previous occasion when she had crashed through the barbed wire and cut herself so badly.

Joe and Maria were very concerned. Every day for more than a week, Maria bathed the wound and put on an antiseptic cream.

Beauty was left with two scars, one old one on her shoulder and a new one, still a vivid purple colour, on her neck.

'It's that old mare,' Joe declared. 'Domino. She'll always find one of the others to pick on.'

'We should sell her off, don't you think?' Maria replied.

'I would, except for one thing.'

Maria understood. 'It's the foal, isn't it,' she said. 'Because the mare's in foal.'

'Next year, when she's had her foal, and weaned him, she'll have to go,' Joe said. 'As sure as I'm standing here!'

After that incident, Joe and Maria did as much as they could to keep the mare and the filly apart. Nevertheless, Domino did her best to worry away at Beauty. There would be no peace for Beauty until the day when she escaped Domino's clutches.

Only Frosty stood Beauty's friend. As he developed, he would push the mare away, and snap his warnings at her.

'I've never seen anything like it,' said Joe. 'I've never seen two horses behave like that.'

'They're almost human,' Maria added.

CHAPTER 18

The Melbourne Cup weekend was the highlight of the year at the Peter Pan Riding Stables.

The Cup was run on the first Tuesday in November, and in Victoria a Public Holiday was given for it.

Many families turned the event into a four-day holiday, spread over the previous three days as well as Cup Day itself.

At the Stables, a four-day pony trek was held, beginning on the Saturday and ending on the following Tuesday.

The riders would have three nights camping in the bush.

Joe and Maria fixed a maximum of ten riders, and the trek was booked out many weeks in advance.

Joe had some doubts about whether to go ahead with the event. There had been no rain for many weeks and already people were talking about an early bushfire season. 'If this weather keeps up, we may have to call the trek off,' he confided to Maria one night. 'We can't have it if a fire gets going up in the Park.'

As yet the drought had not taken full hold. Maria urged Joe to let it go ahead. 'Think of the disappointment if it's called off', she said. 'These families have been making their plans since this time last year.'

In the event, there was a cooler spell in early November, and Joe dropped the matter, though he made sure he had an emergency plan in case a fire broke out after the ride had begun.

The trek began with the usual formalities – the calling-out of the riders and the allocation of horses.

Joe went on, 'If anything goes wrong, your leaders, Frank and Mia, will let me know by phone. If a horse goes lame, I can bring in a replacement within a couple of hours. Take extra care in this dry weather with your campfires.' He ended with his usual instruction: 'Listen to your leaders and do what they say.'

Because of the higher numbers, there were four leaders on this trek. Another man was drafted in to help Frank, Mia and Bob Morrison. The man chosen was Bob Morrison's colleague, Jeff.

'I'm not too sure about him.' said Joe to Maria, 'He's very slack when it comes to the little things, the details, and they can matter a lot on a pony trek like this. But I can't find anyone else.'

Beauty was now trained to saddle and rider, so was chosen for the first time as one of the ten horses for the trek. Frosty was alongside her, while two of the older horses were chosen as pack-horses – the old mare, Domino, and one other.

Beauty, whose legs were still developing, had the youngest and lightest rider.

As the trekkers set out that Saturday morning from the entrance to the National Park, little did they realise the dramatic turn of events that was about to take place.

* * *

The first night saw the party at the old campsite alongside the mountain spring. The horses had travelled well. Beauty had become used to her child-rider, although Frank, always on the alert, noticed signs of flightiness in her as they continued deeper into the Park.

Bob and Jeff were responsible for the high line. Again, they strung ropes between trees and tied the horses to it. Bob took off their bridles and saddles and stacked them under shelter. Meanwhile Jeff loosely tied a halter around the head of each horse and attached it to the high line.

'You know how to do it?' Bob called to his mate.

'Yeah. I've done it before,' came the reply. 'It's easy.' When he had finished he walked away without a backward glance.

The horses were attended to. The tents were put up. The evening meal was over, and the campers, weary after a day in the saddle, had settled down for the night.

By nine o'clock all was quiet. A three-quarter moon had risen and the night was calm. The horses stood quietly in their places.

Without warning, the stillness of the night was broken by a single high-powered rifle-shot.

It came from the hills high above the camp. The sound of the shot echoed round and round the hills.

Then a second shot, but by then pandemonium had broken loose.

The younger children shrieked in alarm.

Frank jumped from his bunk. 'Those shooters!' he shouted. 'Breaking the law!' His concern was for the children, but more so for the horses. Maria and he scrambled from their tent. 'Kangaroo shooters!' Mia muttered. 'Where are the rangers when you need them?'

At the sound of the first shot, Beauty reared in terror and confusion. The memory of those other shootings so near this very spot stabbed into her mind.

She flung her head violently upwards. The halter, so loosely attached by Jeff, ripped off. The filly snorted her freedom, reared up in a mighty pirouette, turned, and set off at full gallop for the bush, away from the direction of the rifle-shot, her hooves thundering into the turf.

Frosty, who had been standing alongside Beauty, tugged with all his strength at his halter. In an instant, it slipped over his ears and fell uselessly to the ground. With a snort he took off after Beauty.

Frank and Maria looked on hopelessly as the two horses, their flanks gleaming in the moonlight, disappeared into the shadows of the bush to the westward.

CHAPTER 19

October and November came and went. The Christmas holidays were in sight.

By now the drought had settled on the land.

The spring rains failed to come. The streams fell away to a trickle. The dams fell to their lowest levels for a decade. There was almost no grass. Janet was feeding hay to her cattle every day.

In December the north winds set in. As the thermometer rose and the wind increased, the danger of bushfire became intense.

Each day, Janet and Molly looked anxiously to the north for signs of smoke in the hills.

They cleared the land around the house and set up a sprinkler system on their roof. A contractor came in to sink a deep bore for water for the animals. They had their plans laid to evacuate the property if a fire were to head towards them.

Each Sunday night, Peter would ring to see how the family was faring. He was ready to drop everything and come to their assistance if fire came.

Molly was optimistic. 'There was some cloud today,' she told her father. 'The wireless says we could get rain at the end of the month.'

Molly was more than ever determined to go back into the National Park and bring back her lost pony, Beauty.

'Those horses,' she said to her father one night, 'I keep worrying about them. What can they be getting to eat?'

Peter consoled her. 'They'll eat the scrub, if they have to,' he said. 'And there'll always be a bit of water up there. They might have to go a distance to find it, that's all.'

Molly and Janet spoke often about the wild horses.

Molly had a strong feeling the horses would still be where she and her father had spotted them from the aeroplane. It was a belief too strong for words. It came from her heart, her instinct. She thought so deeply about the brumbies that a kind of unnatural bond had come to exist between them. She knew beyond reason where they would be when the time came for another mission to rescue Beauty.

Molly was laying her plans for that day.

'As soon as the Christmas holidays come,' she said to her mother, 'then we'll go again. And Dad can come with us this time.'

Molly was sure that her father would be able to locate the valley where the two of them had seen the brumbies from the air. 'I think I can find it,' she said, 'but Dad will know for sure.'

Janet tried to dampen her daughter's enthusiasm.

'I don't think we can go in this weather,' she said. 'If a fire came while we were in the bush there'd be no escape.'

But Molly was not to be put off by that. 'As soon as the rain comes, then we'll go,' she replied.

Janet still wanted to put on the brakes. 'Remember I've got to get time off work, and your father, as well, if he is to come with us,' she added.

'It will work out, you see,' replied Molly. 'We'll open up the gap in the fence again, so we can bring Beauty back through it, and we'll take our molasses and salt lick and some carrots and things like that, and Beauty won't be able to resist them. She'll remember the nice things I used to give her when she was small, and she'll remember me, too.'

'Janet looked wistfully at her daughter. 'Don't forget that Beauty is a year older now. She'll be fully grown. She won't be the same as she was.'

Neither Janet nor Molly had any inkling of what Beauty had been through since the day she broke out from their farm.

They knew nothing of her being stolen from the National Park and badly treated by her captor

They were ignorant of Beauty being sold to some riding stables and trained to be ridden.

They did not know that she had received kindness at the hands of her new owners, but also been the victim of vicious bullying by an older horse.

And little did they know that Beauty had gained a horse friend who protected her as best he could, and who was now running free with her in the high country of the National Park.

CHAPTER 20

Despite the heat and threat of bushfire, Molly asked her friend from further down the road, Prue, to spend Christmas Day with her.

Prue's mother dropped her off early in the morning.

It was too hot to do anything energetic. They spent most of the day lounging on the front veranda of the house. The veranda faced south, and so was out of the sun's direct rays.

At four o'clock there was a phone call from Prue's mother. 'There's a storm coming,' she told Janet. 'The Weather Bureau has put out a warning. It's just been posted on the website.'

'Is this the change we've been longing for?' Janet wondered aloud.

'Maybe,' said Prue's mother. 'They say there may be an electrical storm in the high country. That might bring some rain.'

'Yes,' thought Janet, 'and fire as well.' She had long experience of summer storms in this high country. Too often they came with thunder and lightning but with not a drop of rain.

'I'd better come and pick up Prue,' her mother said, 'in case something bad develops.'

* * *

The storm broke that night. At eight o'clock, Janet and Molly heard the ominous rumbling of thunder to their north.

It crackled round the mountains, bouncing from one rocky hillside to another, then back again. The peals of thunder sounded like a symphony of bassoons.

Janet and Molly watched the sky from their backyard. A dazzling flash of lightning would streak from heaven to earth, then another and another, followed by successive explosions of thunder.

'The mountain giants are throwing the crockery around tonight,' muttered Janet.

'There go the dinner plates,' replied Molly, as a particularly loud crash of thunder reached them.

The sky to the north, already dim at the day's ending, became black with thunder clouds. The lightning flashed like mad devils through these massed pillars of doom.

'Anything could happen tonight,' Janet murmured.

'I'm thinking of the horses,' said Molly. 'They'll be terrified.'

In her imagination she thought of her Beauty cowering away from the hurly-burly, leaning into her mother, Bonny, for protection.

But it was not with her mother that Beauty sought comfort that night. It was with a handsome young dappled colt, newly come with her into this rough and dangerous place.

Beauty pushed her head hard against Frosty as the storm raged about them.

The rest of the mob stood close by.

CHAPTER 21

The fire began late that night.

A tongue of lightning struck the upper branches of a dead tree high up in the Park.

The heat caused the dead dust of the old 'stag' to smoulder.

This was a 'dry' storm. There was no rain to dampen the slow, insidious spread of the hot embers.

Before long the smouldering branch broke off and fell into a mass of wire grass and dead bracken beneath.

It took a long time for the fire to take hold at ground level. But there was a heavy load of sticks and bush debris to feed its voracious appetite.

Down one hillside the flames crept, then raced up the hill opposite.

In the morning the north wind sprang up with particular ferocity. Within two hours the fire front, once tiny, became a roaring furnace, kilometres across.

The news bulletins on wireless and television brought warnings to local residents: "Prepare to implement your fire plan". Later, more urgent warnings came through by text and telephone: "You must leave now".

By mid-afternoon, all Janet and Molly could see to their north was a menacing sky purple with smoke-haze. Cinders began to fall around the house.

Janet rushed to open the gates to the paddocks so the cattle would not be trapped.

Molly rushed around the house making sure the windows were tightly closed. The two of them stashed their precious belongings in the car. These had been ready in boxes for many days, since the fire threat began. Janet threw in a heap of sheets and blankets.

Just at the moment they were about to drive away, Peter's car swung into the yard. He had rushed from the coast as soon as he heard of the threat to the up-country regions.

His vehicle skidded to a stop. The three of them, overcome with nervous exhaustion, hugged each other in one mutual embrace.

There was nothing left to do but to get away.

The two vehicles, Janet and Molly in front and Peter behind them, sped down the drive, through the gate on to the main road, and away towards the relative safety of the town.

Their hope was that they could get to the emergency relief centre that had been set up at the High School in town, Molly's own school.

Molly looked behind as the car hit the main road. She wondered if she would ever see her home again. Or would it fall victim to the insatiable flames?

But her thoughts travelled further, to the rugged bushland beyond, to the wild bush horses that had become the most important thing in her life.

'What will they do?' she cried out inside herself. 'How can they escape?'

CHAPTER 22

On the morning of that ghastly day the horses were camped in a gully about half way between the Park boundary and the high peaks above the tree line.

There was Queenie and her foal, the fillies, Pretty and Shaggy, the colts, Scar and Son of Boss, Bonny, and the two who had joined them only weeks earlier, Beauty and her friend Frosty.

Beauty had mixed immediately with them. She had quickly become one of the mob, as she had been many months before. And she was once more reunited with her mother, Bonny.

Frosty, however, who had known life only as a domesticated hack, was still coming to accept his new freedom. It was not so much his being accepted by the other horses as his finding it hard to accept the dramatic change in every part of his daily existence. Now, however, like the others, he was in a high state of nervous excitement.

They were alarmed by the hot north wind that sprang up at first light.

Soon afterwards the first wisp of smoke reached them.

The Boss was the first to raise the alarm. He snorted a warning and pawed at the ground as he rounded the others into a tight circle.

By nine o'clock, as the smoke thickened, the mob started to move.

Heads high in the air, nostrils splayed, taking in the nauseous smoke, the big stallion led them downhill. But where could they go? Where did this horrid smoke come from? It was everywhere. Where could they escape from it? It had no form, no front, nothing to run from.

Until they heard the crackling of flame.

It was now late in the morning. The fire demon was hard upon them. The flames roared through the undergrowth. It climbed up the bark of the trees. It leapt from tree-top to tree-top. The hot breath of the wind scorched every living thing.

All the horses could do was run madly. Downhill first, then across the slope of a hill, only to find that the flames had cut them off.

The other way … but the flames were there too!

Across gullies, through boggy mudholes, over gravel scree-slopes, leaping fallen trees, they careered, the distraught Boss at their head, the others following, eyes straining, lungs bursting.

Beauty stumbled, recovered, fell again, dropped behind, then, as the mob wheeled to the left, cut through the angle and re-joined them.

Frosty, taken with the general hysteria, ran blindly.

Bonny, in foal, staggered. The younger Pretty, also carrying a foal, was at the point of dropping. Queenie herself, her foal at surrender point, was ready to give in.

Only The Boss's relentless urging kept them going.

Of a sudden, in a natural open space, The Boss stopped. Stock still. The others crashed and crowded around him. They sucked in huge gulps of air. Their heads hung low to the ground. The sweat poured from them. The foal fell prostrate. Queenie licked at him, but her tongue was dry. Beauty and Frosty found each other, and stood, gasping, head to head.

The roar of the fire filled their ears; the smoke penetrated their lungs; the heat suffocated them.

But The Boss had sensed that this was the way of escape. This spot. The flames continued to roar, on either side, behind them, ahead of them, but not where they were.

The fire had passed them by. The flames had leapt over them. The flat rocky surface here in this spot held nothing to feed the appetite of the all-consuming flames.

The front of the fire roared on, down to the Park boundary, through the paddocks, into the farmland, towards the farmers' homes, devouring some, sparing others, just as this mob of horses had been spared.

As the danger passed, some of the horses lay themselves flat on the ground, others licked at themselves. Frosty came to Beauty and nuzzled her.

Late in the day, with the danger now gone, Queenie led them through the blackened, still-smouldering ground cover, to a pool of water in a narrow defile nearby.

The exhausted, frightened animals drank deeply. The moonrise found them, bunched closely together, some standing, some lying.

All around was stillness, silence.

CHAPTER 23

Thirty or forty people – men, women, and children – were housed in the Emergency Relief Centre while the fire raged to the north. The local CWA branch provided food, and the Red Cross and the local churches sent people to help.

It was an agonising two days for them all. For Molly and her family, they had no way of knowing whether their home had survived the flames, nor their herd of cattle.

It was easier for Peter. He volunteered to help with the local CFA Branch, and although he wasn't trained to take part in their front-line work, he helped at the depot. He had work to do, and his mind was distracted from what might have happened at the farm.

Exhausted crews of fire-fighters would return from the fire front, and fresh crews replace them. But despite Peter's pleas none could tell him whether the house had been saved.

Everyone at the Relief Centre was desperate to get back home. But the roads were still unsafe, they were told. The fire was not yet under control. Emergency vehicles needed unhindered access throughout the fire zone. Burnt trees along the roadsides might come crashing down.

Late on the second night, however, good news came through. With the aid of aeroplanes and helicopters using water and chemical retardants, the fire was sufficiently subdued for families to return to their homes. The roads were safe again.

At seven o'clock the next morning, Janet, Peter, and Molly set out in Janet's car to discover their fate. Their hearts were in their mouths.

Peter's car was left in town. The three of them needed to be together on this fateful journey

All three were strangely silent, each deep in their own thoughts.

Nearing their home, they came into fire-blackened country. The grass in the paddocks had mostly escaped but the trees along the sides of the road had acted as a pipeline for the flames. The trees stood gaunt and black, some still smoking.

Molly feared for the worst.

They passed Prue's farm. Saved! The flames had been merciful. Molly said a silent prayer of thanks.

Now another property. The paddocks were black. The fence posts were burnt. The house was gone. Only a smouldering heap of twisted timber and iron stood where a loved family home once stood.

The little family now feared the worst. All hope was evaporating.

They came to the bend in the road that took them within sight of their own place.

A desolate scene met their eyes. It was as if a giant hand had taken a paint-brush and smeared the whole landscape with a death-like inkiness.

Their front gate was gone. The front fence was gone. The paddocks were burnt to a cinder. There was no sign of the cattle.

But in the middle of this scene of desolation – could they believe their eyes? – their house stood, unharmed.

Peter, almost in disbelief, dashed from the car.

'Water-bombed!' he yelled. 'Water-bombed! There's no other way!'

The fire had come to the very edge of their garden, within twenty metres of the house itself. But it was untouched.

'Water-bombed!' Peter shouted again. 'Couldn't be anything else! They couldn't save the farm, but the planes have saved the house. Thank God!'

'Thank God, indeed,' echoed Janet.

As for Molly, she was crying quietly in relief.

Or was it because she carried in her mind's eye the destruction she had seen all around, their neighbours losing all they had, the heartache of the whole dead and blackened scene?

Or because she was able to see the devastation of the forest above her? The National Park was a desolate, smoking ruin.

What chance did any living thing have to survive?

Janet made a quick calculation of the damage. Their hayshed was burnt, with all their hay, though the machinery shed, close to the house, was intact. Half their fencing had been lost.

But the cattle had survived. A farmer further towards town rang to say he had found them on the road, a frightened and bedraggled mob, and had turned them into one of his own paddocks till they could be retrieved.

Janet breathed a sigh of relief. 'Thank goodness I opened those gates,' she said.

That night an earnest consultation took place between Janet and Peter.

Molly had gone early to her bedroom, though Janet noticed that her light stayed on till late.

At ten o'clock, Janet came into Molly's room. 'Time for us all to get some sleep,' she said.

But Janet didn't put the light off. Instead she sat on Molly's bed.

She was quiet for a little while, then she took Molly's hand. 'Your dad and I have been doing some sums. We think we can struggle through here on the farm. The insurance will cover some of the damage. And you wouldn't want to leave here, would you?' Janet asked.

'I'll never leave here,' Molly said, softly.

There was silence for a minute or two. Then Janet spoke again.

'There's something else,' she began. 'Your father and I …,' and here she paused. Molly knew something very important was coming.

Janet began again. 'Well, you know how Peter has been working down on the coast all this time.'

Molly remained silent.

'And living down there,' Janet went on. 'Well, he's going to come home now. Every weekend.'

'Here?' said Molly, unbelievingly.

"Yes, here. We've talked it through. He's coming home to be your father once again.'

There was no need for words.

Molly lay back in her bed. A deep peace entered her entire body.

After waiting a while, Janet left the room and switched off the light. Peter was waiting by the door.

Molly was in a confusion of mind. How could good things and bad things happen at the same time?

Her father was coming home. The family was complete once again. But there in the hills beyond her farm was a mob of beautiful wild horses where half of her heart lay.

Was Beauty alive still?

Or had she succumbed to the flames?

CHAPTER 24

Things were different now, back at the Peter Pan Riding Stables.

Joe and Maria had learnt some lessons. They would never again take children into the National Park for their pony treks. There were too many risks. Instead, they would use the back roads near their property. There was so little traffic there, they were perfectly safe, and they could put up warning signs for the few drivers who did come along.

They were recovering from the disaster of losing their two best young horses. At the time of Beauty and Frosty's breaking away, they had been able to take two replacement mounts there within a couple of hours, and the trek had been resumed safely.

The loss of these two young horses was a severe blow. They were valuable animals, for a start. But, more than that, Joe had hoped they would be the backbone of his breeding stock over the next few years.

The old mare continued her nasty habits. Having lost Beauty, her favourite target, she soon found others to persecute. Joe and Maria were more determined than ever that after she had her foal the next spring, she would be turned out. 'If I can't find a buyer,' Joe said, 'we'll just put her in the back paddock where she'll have no one to mistreat. She can end her days there.'

Joe and Maria retained the services of Frank and Mia. In fact, as more and more children came to use their horses, Mia and Frank found employment at the Stables most weekends. Mia's soft nature won the trust of the ponies. 'She's a good one,' Maria said of her.

As for the two other men, Joe quickly made up his mind to finish them up. 'I've had enough of that Bob Morrison,' Joe said to Maria one evening, after he had seen Bob belting a pony with a length of rope when it refused a training routine. 'We don't want his sort here. And I've always been doubtful about where he gets his horses from. I'm not sure he's an honest man.'

And Joe could never overlook Jeff's part in the escape of his two favourite horses. 'If he'd taken more care that night, we might still have them,' he said. Joe wasn't the sort to sack a man on the spot, but back at the Stables he told Jeff to finish up at the end of the week. 'I like a man who really cares for his horses,' Joe confided to Frank later on. 'A good horseman thinks more of his horse's welfare than his own, and that Jeff never gave a second thought to any of them.'

CHAPTER 25

By the time autumn arrived, things had changed for the little mob of brumbies.

The furious gallop to escape the flames of the fire proved too much for Queenie's young foal. She lingered for some weeks, but her mother had hardly any milk to give her. The fire had burnt almost all the feed available. One day, the foal went off by herself, lay down and died.

As autumn approached, the colt, Scar, became increasingly restless. The Boss saw him as a potential rival. One day they fought, and Scar was driven away. He would no doubt seek the company of another mob further away in the Park, or he would perhaps return to take away one of the females from his own mob.

The fire generated some shrubby growth, though there was little nourishment in it. The remaining horses lost condition. Their ribs showed starkly through their skin. Their dull coats and glassy eyes showed their weakness. Their muscles weakened to the point that they could hardly move at anything more than a shambling pace. Yet, somehow they survived.

Beauty and Frosty were now freely accepted into the mob. They, too, became emaciated, although they joined the group in better condition than the others, so they remained a little stronger. Did they recall the biscuits of sweet hay that were brought to them in the days of their captivity? And the cool, deep troughs of water? Those days seemed gone for ever.

And still the autumn rain failed to come. A few local sprinkles brought the merest green tinge to some of the valleys.

One day, with her instinctive cunning, Queenie led the herd to a place higher in the Park. It was a spot they knew well. There was water here, and the fire had spared the ground cover. There was the merest green haze of growth in some of the pockets of deeper soil.

It was the same valley where the herd had been on the day, now distant in their memories, when a plane had flown low overhead, and they had bolted for the trees.

CHAPTER 26

It was at this time that Molly had her great new idea.

Her mind had never left the mob of horses running wild in the Park. She continued to think of them night and day. 'What will they find to eat?' she asked her mother over and over again. But her mother had no answer.

For many weeks she and her mother and father were pre-occupied with their own troubles, as they worked desperately to overcome the difficulties the fire had caused them. There was fencing to be organised, hay for the stock to be brought in, the cattle to be returned and settled down.

It was the last week of term before the Easter holidays. A truckload of hay had just arrived at the farm, and it was while watching the men unloading it that Molly had her inspiration.

'That's what they need!' Molly suddenly called out.

"Who needs what?' Janet replied. She often found it hard to understand Molly's sudden changes of thought.

'The horses! Hay! They must be starving, after the fire.'

Molly was now excited by her own thought. 'We could take hay to the horses! In the Park! To Beauty! And the others!' Molly jumped up and down.

Janet was quite shaken by what Molly had said. At first the idea seemed preposterous – to carry hay into the National Park, up those steep slopes, across that rugged terrain.

Janet was always cautious about Molly's often over-enthusiastic ideas.

But then again, it was not impossible. Janet hesitated.

'Yes, maybe,' she replied eventually. 'Maybe it can be done. Let's think about it.'

But Molly required no further thinking. By nightfall she had worked out a detailed plan to "Save the Horses". That became her slogan. She made a banner and posted it on her bedroom door: "SAVE THE HORSES!"

It was principally Beauty that Molly wanted to save, of course, but she believed that feeding the horses would help the mob to survive as well as bringing not only Beauty, but Bonny back to her as well.

'Here's how it would work, Mum,' she explained over breakfast the next morning. 'On Saturday, when Dad is home, the three of us will take a bale of hay, one of those small ones, divide it into three, and carry it up to where the horses are, and leave it for them. It won't matter if we don't even see them. And we can be back home in time for tea.'

Janet saw some merit in the plan. The horses' sense of smell would lead them to the hay. 'But I don't think we can take a day off working on the farm,' she said.

'Just for one day,' Molly insisted. 'Please! Join the "Save the Horses" Club!'

'Maybe, then,' said Janet.

Molly rushed on. 'Then, each time we go, we leave the hay a little bit further down the mountain, a little bit closer to our place. We'll get them to come down near the fence after a while, and when she's so close then I can bring Beauty home with me. I'm sure she'll come'.

It seemed a madcap scheme to Janet. But it could just work, she mused. 'All right,' she finished up. 'I'll ring Peter about it'.

Molly felt sure she had won the day. She went off to school happily making plans for the next Saturday's adventure.

*   *   *

They divided their bale of hay into three unequal portions. Peter had the biggest and Molly the smallest. They were tied on the top of their back-packs with baling twine. 'We look like three walking haystacks,' Janet laughed.

Peter also carried their supplies for lunch. Each had a water bottle.

They headed straight for the hidden valley where the horses had been on the day of the aeroplane flight several months before. It was some two kilometres from the farm.

*　　*　　*

They sighted the horses after two hours of toiling up the steep and rocky slopes.

Suddenly, they were there, two hundred metres above them, staring down at the intruders. The horses stood for a moment, then, at a signal from Queenie, turned back in a jumble towards the trees behind them.

'That's it,' cried Peter. 'See, they're already going.'

Molly whipped out her binoculars, but, too late. The horses had vanished.

Molly threw down her back-pack. 'Was Beauty there? Did you see her?' she called to the others.

But no one could be sure. 'There was so little time,' said Janet. 'I did see a chestnut. Perhaps it was Beauty, or maybe Bonny. They'd be the same size now.'

'There was a grey one,' Peter added. 'That's the one that stood out. He's a different colour from the rest.'

Molly was deeply disappointed, but Peter, who knew the ways of horses, cheered her up.

'We'll spread out the hay here. You can bet your life that when we've gone they'll come after it. Those horses could smell a feed from a hundred kilometres!'

'But they won't come till we're well out of sight,' said Janet.

Molly looked up the slope to where she had last seen the mob of horses. 'Next time!' she called wistfully.

'Next time,' echoed her father. 'And next time, we'll leave the hay closer to home.' He turned to Molly. 'Just like you said,' he added.

'That will save some of our aching muscles, at any rate!' added Janet, with a laugh.

And the three of them began their slow descent down the mountain.

CHAPTER 27

Every Saturday the "SAVE THE HORSES" team went into action.

Sometimes all three, sometimes just Molly and Janet, and sometimes Molly and Peter, would leave home early in the day, as much hay as they could possibly carry on their backs, and head through their boundary fence, up the steep slopes towards where the mob had last been seen.

With each visit, they found the horses less and less suspicious. They remained at a distance, however, under shelter, too far away for Molly to pick out either Bonny or Beauty.

The bush horses found the hay irresistible, but they also were coming to realise that these visitors meant them no harm, only good.

On the fifth occasion, some of the horses came out from their cover and stood, half in the open, and half in the shelter of the trees, still in the distance, watching the intruders as they spread out the hay on the ground.

Peter brought out some small blocks he had broken off a salt-lick he'd carried with him. 'They'll die for this!' he said, as he scattered them around.

Molly was straining to make out her beloved Beauty. She still didn't know whether she would be there or not, or even whether she was alive or dead. She peered into the distance, screwing up her eyes, squinting up the hill-slope.

Her hand went to her back-pack. Then, with a thud she realised the worst. 'Mum! We've left the binoculars at home!' she shrieked, and stamped her foot in frustration and anger at herself.

Her parents were also peering up the hill with all their might. 'I can see that grey one again,' Peter called.

But before they could make out any more, the horses retreated into the shelter of the bush.

'That's all we can do,' said Peter. 'They're still too shy to come down to us. We'll leave the hay to do its work. And the salt-lick.'

They turned to go. 'You see,' Molly said. 'It's working. My plan is working. Just wait. Soon they'll let us go right up to them.'

And Janet had to admit that her daughter's plan could perhaps succeed.

* * *

The day came that the brumbies were waiting for the hay party to arrive.

They even came towards them, across the open space, stopping for a while and then edging forwards again.

Molly and Janet and Peter stopped in their tracks as Queenie led the horses forward.

'There's Beauty!' Molly stifled her shout of delight. 'Mum, there's Beauty! See her! See there, at the back! See the white smudge!'

'There's Bonny, too,' Janet whispered back, and pointed her out to Peter.

'She's in foal,' Peter joined in. 'Can you see? Bonny's in foal.'

'And Beauty's so tall,' Molly went on. 'And strong.'

Peter took off his pack and began to spread hay in front of the herd. Janet and Molly did the same. Peter threw out pieces of salt-lick that he had smeared with molasses.

Slowly at first, but then, losing their last vestige of fear, the horses began to eat hungrily from the little feast set before them.

As they snuffled at the last scraps of hay, Molly began to move gently amongst them.

She came to Beauty.

There was a look of fondness in Beauty's eyes. She bowed her head towards Molly.

Molly reached out her hand and stroked Beauty's forehead, roughing it upwards just as she used to do when Beauty was a foal.

She saw the scar on Beauty's shoulder where she had broken through the barbed wire all those months ago, and then the other wound on her neck where the mare, Domino, had attacked her. 'What have you been doing to yourself, you poor thing?' she murmured.

Molly noticed a striking pale grey colt standing close to Molly's hindquarters.

He came to stand beside Beauty, and Molly stroked his forehead, too.

Janet and Peter stood back in amazement.

Molly murmured soft words to her old friend, then slowly walked the few paces back to where her back-pack lay on the ground.

She took from it a nylon rope and carried it back to where Beauty remained motionless.

Gently caressing Beauty's face and shoulders, Molly slipped it over the filly's head.

Beauty gave no resistance. The grey, Frosty, pushed himself forward, and Molly spoke soothing words to him also.

Without a word, Molly turned and began to lead her old friend down the hill towards the farm, to the place where Beauty had once known love and security.

Frosty, unrestrained, walked freely by her side.

Janet and Peter picked up their back-packs.

Janet looked up to see Bonny, large in foal, standing farther up the hill, close to The Boss. Janet took a step towards her, but with a shake of her head, Bonny turned away, and with The Boss bedside her, moved swiftly away, towards the shelter of the trees.

'She's saying goodbye,' Peter said to his wife. 'I think Bonny has truly become one with the wild horses. We'll have to let her go to them.'

Janet understood. 'Yes,' she replied. 'Bonny will never again know bit or bridle.'

Janet paused. 'She will spend her life now with these free spirits of the mountain.'

Molly's parents turned to begin their walk down the mountain.

Behind them the mob of brumbies gathered as silent spectators.

Ahead of them, Molly led her old friend down the rough hillside track towards the farm.

Frosty followed faithfully at Beauty's heels.

CHAPTER 28

Beauty is standing in the paddock at Molly's farm.

Behind her is the fence that separates the farm from the National Park.

There, too, is the gap in the fence through which Molly has just led her.

Molly stands with Beauty. Frosty is alongside.

Molly removes the rope from around the horse's neck.

'You're home now,' she says. 'Home again. No more hunger, no more fear,' and caresses Beauty's head in her hands.

Frosty draws back. He turns and looks into the bush he has come from. He sniffs the air.

Janet and Peter watch from a distance.

They see sudden movement in the hills. The mob have followed Beauty and Frosty down from the mountain and are standing in open view in the Park, on the far side of the boundary fence.

Beauty catches some of Frosty's nervousness and energy.

She becomes uneasy. There is sweat on her face.

Molly senses that there is a tug-of-war in Beauty's heart.

She lets go of the horse's head.

For so long Molly has sought only one thing – to have Beauty back with her.

In a flash of understanding, she comes to a new realisation.

If she truly loves Beauty, then she must give Beauty her own free will. Beauty can only be hers if she comes freely to her.

For a moment the scene is frozen in time.

Janet and Peter stand apart as onlookers.

Frosty snorts and shakes his mane.

Molly stands at Beauty's head as the horse looks deep into the girl's eyes.

Into this moment of decision comes a high-pitched braying call from the bushland beyond.

It is The Boss calling his herd to come if they will.

Frosty rears high in the air. He snorts a rallying cry to Beauty, turns, and canters off a dozen metres towards The Boss's summons. He stops, turns, and paws the ground.

Beauty gives Molly a last, lingering look, as if to say, 'Please forgive me. I must go where I am called to go.'

Molly will never forget that look.

Beauty turns, arches her back, and takes off headlong across the paddock, through the gap, into the forest, Frosty beside her, to freedom.

For a moment Molly stands shock still, glowing with a sad thrill that she has done what was right to do. Then she softly murmurs into the distance, 'Goodbye my dear friend. You are free now. Free for ever. Now I know. You were born for freedom.'

There is a blur of colour in the hills, one last call from the boss stallion, a thunder of hooves, and the mob disappears into the forest depths.

*   *   *

Peter and Janet come to Molly and put their arms around her shoulders.

The three turn towards home. The setting sun is casting a rosy glow on the western windows.

'I was wrong, wasn't I,' Molly says to her mother and father, 'to want Beauty just for myself?'

'Not wrong,' says Janet. 'But now you have chosen the right.'

'Come,' says Peter, sharply. 'Time for tea!'

130

THE END

www.ingramcontent.com/pod-product-compliance
Lightning Source LLC
Chambersburg PA
CBHW021433110726
47901CB00008B/2403